Best Best Friends

Margaret Chodos-Irvine

HARCOURT, INC.

Orlando Austin New York San Diego Toronto London

Manufactured in China

Clare and Mary are best friends.

Every day, when they get to preschool,
they give each other big hugs.

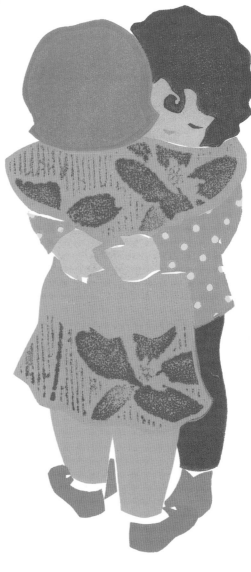

They sit together at storytime.

When they go outside to play,
they always hold hands.

"You are my best best friend,"
Clare tells Mary.

"You are my best best friend, too,"
Mary tells Clare.

But today is Mary's birthday.

Mary gets big hugs from everybody.

She sits next to the teacher at storytime,

and when it's time to go outside,

Mary gets to be first in line.

Clare has to wait her turn.

At snacktime, there's a party for Mary.
There are cupcakes with pink frosting
and pink sprinkles on top.
Everyone sings "Happy Birthday" to Mary,

and Mary gets to wear a golden birthday crown.

At playtime, Clare says,
"If it was my birthday, I would have yellow
cupcakes with yellow sprinkles.
Yellow is prettier than plain old pink."

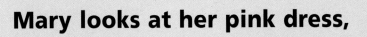

Mary looks at her pink dress,

pink socks,

pink shoes,

and

pink

underpants.

"You're not nice!"
Mary tells Clare.

"You're not, either!"
Clare tells Mary.

"I'm mad at you more!"
yells Clare.

"YOU ARE NOT

MY FRIEND!"

So Mary goes and plays with Kaitlin,

and Clare goes and plays with Ben.

But after naptime, Clare draws a picture

and gives it to Mary.
"Happy birthday, Mary,"
says Clare.

Mary looks at the picture.

"Let's build a teddy bear castle," says Mary.
"We can take turns being Teddy Bear Queen."

"Shiny gold is really the best color of all,"
Mary says.

And Clare agrees.

When it's time to go home,
they give each other big hugs.

"You are my best best BEST friend,"
Clare tells Mary.

"You are my best best BEST friend, too,"
Mary tells Clare.

"SEE YOU

TOMORROW! "

For Clare and Mary

and best friends everywhere

Requests for permission to make copies of any part of the work should be mailed to the following address: Permissions Department, Harcourt, Inc., 6277 Sea Harbor Drive, Orlando, Florida 32887-6777.

www.HarcourtBooks.com

Library of Congress Cataloging-in-Publication Data
Chodos-Irvine, Margaret.
Best best friends/written and illustrated by Margaret Chodos-Irvine.
p. cm.
Summary: Mary and Clare do everything together at preschool, but Mary's birthday celebration puts a strain on the girls' friendship.
[1. Best friends—Fiction. 2. Friendship—Fiction. 3. Nursery schools—Fiction. 4. Schools—Fiction.] I. Title.
PZ7.C44625Be 2006
[E]—dc22   2005002251
ISBN-13: 978-0152-05694-0   ISBN 10: 0-15-205694-7

First edition
A C E G H F D B

The illustrations in this book were created using a variety of printmaking techniques on Rives paper.
The display type was created by Margaret Chodos-Irvine and Judythe Sieck.
The text type was set in Frutiger.
Color separations by Bright Arts Ltd., Hong Kong
Manufactured by South China Printing Company, Ltd., China
This book was printed on totally chlorine-free Enso Stora Matte paper.
Production supervision by Pascha Gerlinger
Designed by Judythe Sieck